Friend on Freedom River

Written by Gloria Whelan

Illustrated by Gijsbert van Frankenhuyzen

Sleeping Bear Press

310 North Main Street, Suite 300
Chelsea, MI 48118
www.sleepingbearpress.com

© 2004 Thomson Gale, a part of the Thomson Corporation.

Thomson, Star Logo and Sleeping Bear Press are trademarks
and Gale is a registered trademark used herein under license.

Printed and bound in Canada.

10 9 8 7 6 5 4 3 2 1

Library of Congress Cataloging-in-Publication on file.

ISBN: 1-58536-222-0

For Moira

GLORIA

Illustrator's Acknowledgments

I have met many new people while creating this book and am grateful for their help and friendship.

To mother and daughter, Brenda and Amber Jones—Your excitement and animation made painting you so much fun. To Samual Steel (who could go into theater)—Your expressions and poses were absolutely perfect. To mother and son, Lisé and Pete Dibert—Thank you for putting up with all the retakes. To Becky Schwarz (a.k.a. Stella Marie from *The Legend of the Teddy Bear* book) and Tom Schneider—People always feel welcome in your home.

Special thanks to Cindy Darden for help in finding my models. Thanks to Tom and Linda Wood for allowing a stranger to borrow their boat. And finally, my appreciation goes to the National Underground Railroad Freedom Center in Cincinnati, Ohio. Visiting the museum truly inspired me.

—*Gijsbert*

Author's Note

It is estimated that 40,000 slaves traveled Michigan's Underground Railway. For many of the slaves the road to freedom led through Detroit and across the Detroit River to Canada.

To commemorate those perilous journeys a "Gateway to Freedom" monument stands on Detroit's Hart Plaza Riverfront Promenade. The 12-foot bronze monument depicts eight figures looking across the Detroit River to Windsor, Ontario in Canada.

Across the Detroit River on the Windsor Civic Esplanade, the 22-foot "Tower of Freedom" monument, with its bronze "Flame of Freedom," celebrates Canada's proud part in the Underground Railway.

—*Gloria*

Louis watched the last of the mallard ducks lift off. Soon ice would seal the Detroit River. He turned over the fishing boat to protect it from the snows. It was what his father had always done. His father had gone north for the winter to work in the logging camps.

Before his father left he told Louis, "Son, you'll be in charge of the farm. If you don't know what to do, just do what you think I would have done."

The icy December wind shook the willow boughs and stripped the leaves from the pear trees. Louis's grandparents had brought the pear trees with them when they came from France to America. Downstream in Detroit the steamboats and schooners were racing winter to the sea.

There was a rustle in the alder bushes.
Louis thought, *A deer or a fox*.

A voice whispered, "Are you a friend?"

Louis was so startled he dropped the boat.
Those words meant only one thing:
runaway slaves.

He answered with the words his father had taught him long ago, words that were a sign to the slaves that they had found friends.

"What do you seek?"
"Freedom."
"Have you got faith?"
"I have hope."

A black woman wrapped in a tatter of a shawl stepped from the bushes. A small girl clung to her. A little apart stood a boy, Louis's age, 12 or 13 years old.

"God bless you," the woman said. "I'm Sarah, my girl is Lucy, and my boy is Tyler. They told us at the Baptist church in Detroit your daddy would help us. The slave catchers from Kentucky are on our trail like bloodhounds. We got to hurry across this river to Canada where a slave is free forever."

Louis knew how upset his mother would be about his trying to cross the river on a night like this. His mother had begged his father to stop carrying slaves across the river. She had warned, "The new Fugitive Slave Law means jail for anyone helping slaves escape."

Over and over his father had taken the chance, asking, "How can I see some soul sent back to slavery?"

"My father isn't here," Louis said. "There's ice on the river and the wind is strong. It's a three hour pull."

"No water's too cold and no wind is too strong for us, child," Sarah said. "We already crossed two rivers, but the Detroit River is freedom's river. It's our last chance. Our master sold away these children's daddy. They were going to sell away Tyler just like he was no different from a horse or a cow. If you don't take us, we might as well jump in and drown ourselves."

The boy was scowling at Louis. "I bet I could row that boat across the river," he said.

The boy's challenge stung Louis. "No you couldn't," Louis said. "You got to know the currents and the shoals."

The woman was shivering. The little girl was crying without making a sound. Louis thought, *She had to learn how to cry so no one could hear her.*

Louis knew what his father would do.

"Wait here," he said.

The heat from the farmhouse kitchen wrapped around Louis like a warm coat. A kettle hung over the glowing coals. He sniffed the aroma of his favorite whitefish stew. Louis had caught the whitefish himself.

"Supper is nearly ready, Louis," his mother said.

"I'll be done with the boat in a minute, Mama. I just want to get a scarf."

In the cubbyhole that was his bedroom Louis opened the window and threw out the quilt from his bed, along with a sweater and a jacket.

Then he returned to the kitchen.

Singing at the top of his voice,
Louis danced his mother
around the table.

Alouette, gentille alouette,
Alouette, je te plumerai
je te plumerai le tete,
et le tete
Alouette

While she was laughing and dizzy from
the dance, he sneaked some pan de chocolat
she had set out to cool.

At the door he turned to her. "Don't worry, Mama, if it takes me a while. Darkness is just daylight turned inside out."

She smiled at him, "That's just what your father always says."

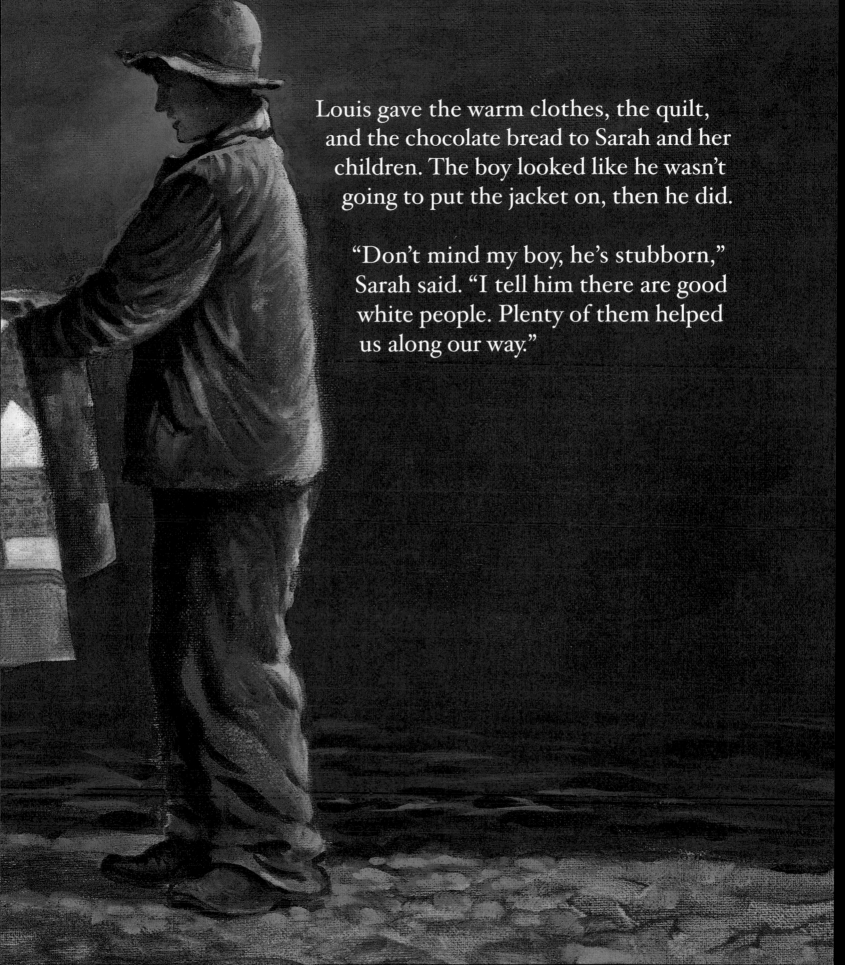

Louis gave the warm clothes, the quilt, and the chocolate bread to Sarah and her children. The boy looked like he wasn't going to put the jacket on, then he did.

"Don't mind my boy, he's stubborn," Sarah said. "I tell him there are good white people. Plenty of them helped us along our way."

Together the two boys pushed the skiff into the water, breaking a thin skin of ice. They held the boat steady while Sarah and Lucy climbed in.

"You sure you can row a boat?" Louis asked Tyler.

"I'm sure. I rowed the boat for Master Harmon when
he went cat fishin'. I rowed him all over Mud Lake."

Louis and Tyler slipped the oars into the
locks. Like a hand reaching up out of the water
the strong current grabbed hold of the skiff. The
river that was such a friend to Louis in the daytime
was a dangerous stranger at night.

"To fight the current we got to paddle upstream as we
paddle across," Louis said. The icy wind stung their faces.
The light from the farmhouse faded.

"How did you get here?" Louis asked Sarah.

"We crossed the Ohio River and come station
to station on the Underground Railway."

"We followed the North Star," Lucy said.

"They sent big dogs sniffing and growling
after us," Tyler said.

Sarah said, "There were kind folk took
us in, hungry, and sent us off full."

The boat shuddered as it plowed through
the thin ice. In the daytime Louis had the
gulls and the other fishermen to keep
him company, but in the winter night
it seemed to Louis the four of them
were the only people left on earth.
Louis's teeth were chattering and
his fingers were numb. Sarah
held Lucy close to protect
her from the wind.

The light from the farmhouse had long since disappeared but now another light wavered on the river. It was the lantern of a patrol boat. Louis felt as if he had swallowed a piece of the ice. If they were discovered, Louis would be sent to jail. Sarah and her children would be sent back to slavery.

"Stop rowing," Louis whispered to Tyler. "We got to be quiet."

As soon as they stopped rowing, their boat began drifting away from Canada. The voices of the men carried across the water as the patrol boat swept by. The wake from the patrol boat splashed against the skiff, but the boat's lantern didn't catch them.

When the patrol boat was out of hearing the boys began to row again. Their arms ached from trying to make up the distance they had lost.

Tyler was as worried as Louis. To break the silence he asked, "What kind of fish you catch in this river?"

"Whitefish, herring, perch, sturgeon. My papa caught a sturgeon that weighed 80 pounds."

"That's a big fish. You got to be strong to catch it. You got to be smart to catch a catfish. The best thing is just to put on a heavy sinker and let some crawlers bump along the bottom of the lake."

The wind was against them and the ice was thickening.
For every foot they gained, the boat seemed to slip back
a foot into the black water. He had never been so cold.

Louis wished he could ask his papa if he had done the
right thing to risk their lives.

Sarah began to sing and the children joined her.

O Lord, O my Lord, keep me from sinkin' down
I tell you what I mean to do
Keep me from sinkin' down
Sometimes I'm up, sometimes I'm down
Keep me from sinkin' down
Sometimes I'm almost on the ground
Keep me from sinkin' down
I look up yonder and what do I see?
I see the angels beckonin' me
Keep me from sinkin' down

After a minute Louis sang, too. The wind tossed the words
back at them and they sent them back into the wind.

They all saw the light at the same time.
"That another patrol boat?" Tyler whispered.

But the light stayed still.

"That's Canada!" Louis shouted.

He and Tyler pulled on the oars. They jumped
out and dragged the skiff onto the shore.

Louis pounded on the door of a nearby farmhouse. He held his breath. What if they were turned away?

A startled man and woman hurried them inside. When everyone was warmed and fed, they urged Louis to stay.

"You can't go back tonight," the man said.

"I have to. Mama will know the boat's gone. If I don't come back she'll think I drowned for sure."

Sarah threw her arms around Louis. Lucy hugged his leg. The two boys shook hands. "I'll come over this summer and we'll get us a sturgeon," Louis promised.

Then Louis left them to their new freedom.

The cold wind stung his face. Over and over Louis had to break the ice with his paddle. His hands were so cold he could hardly hold the oars. The boat was lighter now and easier to row. It was also a lot easier to be afraid when you were alone. He wished Tyler were there.

To keep himself company he began to sing,
"Keep me from sinkin' down." He could almost
hear Sarah and her children joining in.

On the distant shore a light broke into the
darkness. This time it was his name that came
to him on the wind. He dug the oars into the
water, pushing aside the ice.

His mother was waiting on the shore. Her arms were around him.

He told her about Sarah and Lucy and Tyler.

"When Papa comes back," Louis said, "I'll tell him, 'Papa, I did what I thought you would do.'"

Gloria Whelan

Gloria Whelan is a poet and the award-winning author of many children's books including *Homeless Bird* for which she received the National Book Award. Born in Detroit, she lived a few blocks from where she situated *Friend on Freedom River*. It is her second children's picture book with Sleeping Bear Press. She wrote *Jam & Jelly by Holly & Nellie*, also illustrated by Gijsbert van Frankenhuyzen. Ms. Whelan lives with her husband, Joe, in the woods of northern Michigan.

Gijsbert van Frankenhuyzen

With the publication of *The Legend of Sleeping Bear*, illustrator Gijsbert van Frankenhuyzen fulfilled his lifelong dream to become a children's book illustrator. In addition to his *Legend* series, his other award-winning titles with Sleeping Bear Press include *The Edmund Fitzgerald: Song of the Bell*, *Jam & Jelly by Holly & Nellie*, *Adopted by an Owl*, and *Saving Samantha*.

Gijsbert is extremely honored to have artwork from his books *Adopted by an Owl* and *The Legend of the Teddy Bear* in the permanent collection of the MAZZA Museum, at the University of Findlay, Ohio. MAZZA is dedicated to promoting literacy by providing educational programs for children and adults through children's books. Gijsbert visits schools throughout the Great Lake states, sharing his love for art and nature. You can visit Gijsbert, his family, and their animals at http://my.voyager.net/robbyn.